Japan

GRADED READERS: INTERMEDIATE

4

Stories by
Tsubota Jōji

translated by

Edmund R. Skrzypczak

JAPAN PUBLICATIONS TRADING CO., LTD.
TOKYO, JAPAN

Published by JAPAN PUBLICATIONS TRADING CO., LTD.
            1-2-1, Sarugaku-chō, Chiyoda-ku,
            Tokyo, 101 Japan

Distributors:
UNITED STATES & CANADA: *JP Trading, Inc., P. O. BOX 610,
   300 Industrial Way, Brisbane, CA 94005.*
BRITISH ISLES & EUROPEAN CONTINENT: *Premier Book Marketing Ltd.,
   1 Gower Street, London WC1E 6HA.*
AUSTRALIA & NEW ZEALAND: *Bookwise International, 54 Crittenden
   Road, Findon, South Australia 5023.*
THE FAR EAST & JAPAN: *Japan Publications Trading Co., Ltd.,
   1-2-1, Sarugaku-chō, Chiyoda-ku, Tokyo, 101 Japan.*

First edition: July 1992 (First printing)

ISBN 0-87040-915-8

Printed in Japan

STORIES BY TSUBOTA JŌJI

Japanese "Characters"
A COLLECTION OF GRADED READERS
FOR STUDENTS OF JAPANESE

ELEMENTARY

    1 Stories by Teramura Teruo (1992)

INTERMEDIATE

    4 Stories by Tsubota Jōji (1992)

ADVANCED

    9 "Chickens" by Mori Ōgai (1992)

Contents

About the Series

*T*ens of thousands of people around the world are now studying Japanese as a foreign language. University departments that offer Japanese are experiencing an unprecedented boom. Japanese is being taught in more and more high schools, and even in primary schools in some parts of the world.

Regardless of their ages, there comes a point when these language students would like to read something in Japanese. If they are beginners, or sometimes even if they have been studying Japanese for two or three years, they still do not know enough kanji to be able to read ordinary books in Japanese. Or, even if the book is mostly in kana, they find the vocabulary too much of a problem. Thus, whether it be kanji that is the obstacle, or vocabulary, their desire to read is frustrated.

The books in this series are designed to meet the needs of such students. They will bridge the gap between the classroom and the library (or bookshop). They will also, I believe, help students consolidate what they learn in the classroom, because stories about situations that can be easily imagined provide tangible examples of words, phrases, and grammatical structures being used in specific contexts. These examples leave deep impressions on the imagination and memory of the reader.

I have tried as much as possible to make the English translation pass muster as English. More important to me, however, was capturing the sense and feeling of the original Japanese, since the idea of having a translation opposite the Japanese text is to aid the student to understand the original. Sometimes capturing the sense of the original meant choosing an English turn of expression that is far from a literal translation of the Japanese, yet is what would be (or could be) used in English to convey the same meaning. After all, the expression, the communication, of meaning is what language is all about, and the reader should learn to grasp the meaning of what is being read.

It is always a problem when devising a series of books such as this, to imagine who the readers will be. Will they be university students? high-school students? second-year students of the language? third-year students? Et cetera. At first I planned to assume that the potential reader would have studied Japanese for two years using one of Anthony Alfonso's structured textbooks, because then I would know, roughly, what vocabulary, grammar, and kanji the reader would have learned. But in view of the enormous boom in Japanese language study in recent years, with the subsequent proliferation of textbooks and diversity in teaching approaches, I decided to aim at a very vague type of reader: someone who had learned some Japanese (formally or informally), knew enough kana to get started, and maybe knew no kanji whatsoever—but who wanted something to read.

For this reason, the first book in this series begins with very few kanji, which appear with the kana readings over them. In subsequent books kanji are introduced more frequently, but in such a way as not, I trust, to overburden the reader. The series as a whole will be divided into three levels of difficulty: elementary, intermediate, and advanced, with the number of kanji increasing gradually with each book in the series.

The Japanese stories chosen for inclusion in this series have been selected because they show aspects of Japan or of Japanese people — sometimes even aspects of the authors who wrote the stories — that reveal the Japanese as people. This is important, because the whole key to understanding people of other countries is the realization that, underneath their different appearances and different ways of doing things, they are people, the same as you, the same as the other people you know.

Finally, the stories were also chosen in the hope that they will prove entertaining. This can be a difficult order to fill sometimes, since what is entertaining to me might not be so to everyone else. Still, most people enjoy meeting interesting people, and it is with this in mind that I have aimed at introducing you to some real "characters." Happy reading!

Edmund R. Skrzypczak

Introduction

The author of the three stories contained in this book was Tsubota Jōji, who was born in 1890 in a small village on the outskirts of Okayama City. He left this village about the age of 17, to begin studies in Tokyo, but for many years he made intermittent trips back to his hometown, sometimes to help his brother in the family business, sometimes to borrow money. After several interruptions, he finally completed his Bachelor's Degree at Waseda University's Department of English Literature in 1915, at the age of twenty-five.

Japan was an exciting place to live during his childhood: railroads were being stretched across the country, telephone lines were going up, those with enough money could buy bicycles, newspapers were being published every day, and some places even had moving picture theaters. But though he spent most of his life in Tokyo, the scenes and people of his childhood remained ever fresh in Mr Tsubota's mind: the rice fields and streams, gardens and insects, steam trains, the other boys in the village, and most especially his two grandfathers—one of whom lived across the road and loved to tell stories, the other of whom lived in a distant village and was an eccentric character who, though not a samurai, liked to imitate the ways of a samurai and liked riding horses.

"Thieves" is one story about this second grand-father. In reading it you will not only meet an interesting old-timer, you will learn something about the boldness of old-time thievery, too. This same grand-father is the main character in the second story as well; his love for horses seems to be the main theme, but his love for people and other "old-time" virtues are perhaps what the author meant to highlight in the old man.

Tsubota Jōji lived through the second World War. The thought-control police were so quick to pounce on anyone who wrote anything that could be interpreted as criticism of the government or the military, that he gave up writing new stories, even stories for children, during the war and spent his time reworking the old Japanese folktales into modern Japanese. "Dreams," the second story in this book, was published in 1948. Even though the war had ended, writers were still careful about what they said. You will better understand what the first part of the story is referring to, and better appreciate the author's skill in describing it, if you ask yourself what momentous, indeed traumatic, event in Japanese history happened three years before, while in the second part you will find a very carefully worded criticism of the Japanese military.

If you have started this series of readers from the elementary level, the number of new kanji, or perhaps I should say the frequency with which new kanji are introduced, has been stepped up another notch. Still,

I hope I have compensated for this by inserting the *furigana* more often, even over kanji that should be more familiar to most readers. Again, as I mentioned in an introduction to one of the elementary readers, I have tried to err in the direction of too many *furigana* rather than too few.

The first two stories by Tsubota Jōji introduce a large number of words that are rarely heard today, such as the words for flint and tinder or for parts of a horse's riding gear. Also, the story contains mostly description, with very little conversation, so that the user of this book might be tempted to think there is little that can be applied to speaking situations in Japan today. In general, though, the structures of the sentences are simple; this is a feature of Tsubota Jōji's stories for children. Most of the patterns that keep occurring in the first two stories, then, will probably be encountered often by the student of the language, and in that sense are useful in speaking situations.

The third story is written as if spoken by a young boy, and for that reason is quite conversational in style. There is a fairly long communiqué from the authorities quoted towards the end of this story, and this portion is extremely formal, so of course you need not expect ever to have to hear, or speak, such sentences. Aside from this section, though, you will find the sentences are of a type readily spoken, and written, in present-day Japan.

Thieves

TSUBOTA Jōji

どろぼう

　おばあさんのことを、いつも善太は、ただおばあさんおばあさんと呼んでいて、名前のことなど気がつかないでおりました。けれども、聞いて見ると、やっぱり名前はありました。松山お米というのでした。お米と書いても、およねと読むのだそうであります。ふしぎな名前と思って、聞いて見ますと、これには訳がありました。

　おばあさんの生まれたのは、万延元年三月、ちょうど井伊大老が桜田門の外で水戸の浪士に殺されたあの年あの月だったそうであります。あの頃は世の中がとても物騒で、町にも田舎にも方々にどろぼうが出たりしました。

　それである夜のこと、おばあさんのお父さん松山甚七はふと目をさまし、遠いお寺の鐘の音を、何時になるかと数えていました。まだそのときはおばあさんは生まれていなかったと言いますから、安政六年という年でありましょう。松山甚七は門の方で重い足音がするように思えて、床の上に起き上がりました。こんなとき、昔の人は心持を静めるため、まずきせるで煙草を吸うたもので

16

Thieves

Zenta had always called his grandmother "Grandmother" and that's all, and the question of her name hadn't ever occurred to him. But one day he asked, and found out she had a name after all. It was Matsuyama O-Yone. It was written "o-kome," he was told, but pronounced "o-yone." Thinking it a strange name, he asked how she got it, to learn there was a long story behind it.

He was told that his grandmother had been born in March 1860, the same year and the same month that Chief Minister Ii was murdered outside the Sakurada Gate by some masterless samurai from Mito. Social conditions were very unsettled in those days, and thieves were active everywhere, in rural areas as well as in the towns.

One night during those troubled times Grandmother's father, Matsuyama Jinshichi, happened to be awake, counting the gongs of a distant temple bell to find out what time it was. Since this was before Grandmother was born, the year must've been 1859. Matsuyama Jinshichi thought he heard heavy footsteps out by the front gate, and he sat up in bed. At times like this the first thing people in the old days used to do to calm their nerves was have a smoke on

あります。それで甚七じいさんも手さぐりで火打ち石を取り上げ、カッチカッチとすりました。火打ち石には必ずほくちというものがついております。

　石と石とすれ合って出る火花が、そのほくちという布切れのようなものにつくのであります。そしてそれは枯芝についた火のように静かに燃え出すのでありました。で、甚七じいさんは今そのほくちから煙草を吸いつけ、パッパッと二三服吸うと、煙草盆の灰吹の上でコッチコッチと叩きました。それでおじいさんは気が静まって、首を傾けて、外の物音に耳をすましました。どうやら米倉にどろぼうが入ったらしいのです。

　おじいさんは立ち上がって、敷居の上にかけてある弓張提灯に手をかけました。けれども、その夜が九月の十七日で、まだ空にお月さまが照ってることを思うて、提灯を取るのをやめました。それから床の間にかかっている長い刀を手に取り、それを提げて玄関の方へ出て行きました。途中で、次の間に寝ているおばあさんを起こしました。

「おみね、おみね、ちょっと米倉を見てくるぞ。後で栄三を起こしとけ。」

a pipe. Grandfather Jinshichi was no exception: he felt around for his flints, picked them up, and struck them together. With flints you always had what was called tinder.

The sparks that fly when one stone is struck against another land on this tinder, which is like a bit of cloth. This would start smoldering, similar to the way dry grass catches fire. Anyway, old Jinshichi lit his tobacco from this smoldering tinder and had a few puffs on his pipe. Then he tapped the pipe a couple times over the ashpot on his tobacco tray. His nerves now calmed, he cocked his head to one side and listened carefully to the sounds out in the yard. He couldn't say for certain, but it sounded as if thieves had got into the rice shed.

Jinshichi rose to his feet and reached up for the bow-handle paper lantern hanging over the doorway. But then it occurred to him that, since it was the 17th day of the ninth month, the moon would still be out, so he decided he wouldn't need the lantern. Then he took up the long sword that was hanging in the alcove and, with it in hand, headed for the front door. On the way he wakened Grandmother's mother, who was asleep in the next room.

"O-Mine! O-Mine! I'm goin' out to have a look at the rice shed. Later go and wake up Eizō."

　玄関に行くと、おじいさんはまず格子になっている玄関脇の窓の戸をあけました。そこから月の光に照らされた門の方を眺めました。すると、門の戸があいております。その上、ちらっとその戸の陰へ、隠れて行く人影が見えました。そこでおじいさんは大急ぎで、玄関の大戸を開きました。門の方へ駆け出しました。門を出て見ると、どうでしょう、彼方へ沈みかけた月の下の田圃道を、三人の男が駆けて行きます。しかも三人が三人とも一俵ずつ米俵を荷いでおります。これを見るとおじいさんは思わず、右手を刀のつかにかけて、五六間も勢こんで駆け出しました。それから大変な大声でその三人のどろぼうにさけびました。

「こうらぁ、どろぼうめい。米を盗むとは何のことじゃ。」

　すると、どろぼうは思いがけない大声にあわてふためき、まるで今にも転びそうに、ひょろひょろして、互にかち合ったり致しましたが、それでも俵を捨てもせず、まだどんどん逃げて行きました。そこでおじいさんがまたさけびかけました。

「こうらぁ、米どろぼう。俵をそこへ置いとけえ。置かんと馬で追いかけるぞう。追いかけて、刀でぶち切るぞう。」

When he came to the front entrance, the first thing Jinshichi did was open the lattice window to one side of the entrance. From there he looked out toward the front gate, which was brightly lit in the moonlight. The door of the front gate was open. What's more, he caught a brief glimpse of someone ducking behind the door. Jinshichi wasted no time: he unlocked the front door and sprinted for the front gate. When he passed through it, lo and behold, in the light of the moon declining in the distance, he saw three men running down the path through the rice fields. And each of them was carrying on his shoulder a large bag of rice. The sight brought a reflex reaction from Jinshichi: his right hand went to the hilt of his sword and he ran full speed down the path a good ten yards or so. Then in a booming voice he shouted at the three thieves:

"Hey, you thievin' louts!! What's the big idea, stealing rice?!"

Startled by the sudden loud shout, the thieves staggered and bumped into one another, so that they nearly tripped; even so, they didn't dump the rice bags but kept right on running. Whereupon Jinshichi yelled to them a second time:

"Stop, you rice thieves! Leave those bags right there! If you don't put 'em down, I'll chase you down on horseback! I'll chase you down and slice you to ribbons with my sword!"

　すると、どろぼうも正直ものと見えまして、一番後ろの男が俵を道に投げ捨てました。前の二人は然しまだ俵を荷いで、とっととっとと逃げて行きました。それでおじいさんはまた大きな声で呼びかけました。

「こうらぁ、まだ置かんかぁ。置かんと、鉄砲で打ち殺すぞう。」

　馬や刀に怖れなかったどろぼうも、鉄砲は怖ろしいと見えまして、次の男がまた俵を道の上に投げました。それでも残る一俵だけは惜しいと見え、三人でそれを担ぐようにして、とっととっとと逃げて行きました。おじいさんはそれでまた声をかけました。

「こうらあ、こんなに言ってもまだ置かんかあ。命が惜しいのか、惜しゅうないのかあ。」

　どろぼうも、一俵だけは命にもかえられなかったのでしょうか、もう何と言っても捨てもせず、三人で代わる代わる担ぎ上げ、次第に遠くなって行きました。しまいには「よっほっ、よっほっ。」などと掛声をかけているのが幽かに聞こえました。

　そのとき、おじいさんの家の作男、栄三が起きて出て来ました。

「旦那、どうしました。」

There are honest persons even among thieves, it seems, for the man bringing up the rear dumped his bag of rice onto the path. The two men ahead of him, however, still shouldering their bags, trotted on at a brisk pace. This brought another shout from Jinshichi.

"All right, still won't drop it, eh? In that case, I'll shoot you down with my gun!"

Even a thief who isn't afraid of a horse or a sword is afraid of a gun, it seems, because now the next man also threw his bag of rice down on the path. But they seemed loathe to part with the one remaining bag, for all three shouldered it and kept trotting briskly along. This produced still another shout from Jinshichi.

"All right, after all my warnings, you still won't put down the rice, eh? Do you value your lives or don't you?"

Apparently as far as the thieves were concerned that one bag of rice couldn't be traded, even for their lives. Nothing Jinshichi said could make them drop the bag. Taking turns shouldering it, the three gradually put plenty of distance between themselves and Jinshichi. In the end their shouts of "Yoh-ho, yoh-ho" and the like to keep step grew fainter.

At this point Jinshichi's farmhand, Eizō, joined him.

"Master, what's going on?"

「うん、どろぼうを逃がした。おしいことをしたわい。」

「どの辺まで逃げました。」

「うん、あそこだ。俵を担いで行くだろう。」

　二人は月の光に手をかざして、遠い彼方の村の方を眺めました。

「あ、あれなら旦那、馬で追っかけりゃ間に合いますぞ。」

　言うか言わないに、もう栄三は門の中へ駆け込んで、鞍も置かない裸馬を引き出して来ました。

「どうどうどう。」

　はやり立てる馬をなだめ、栄三はそこで馬に飛び乗ろうと致しました。

「待て待て、待て。」

　おじいさんは尻からげをし、手に下げていた刀を腰にさしました。それから栄三の手綱をとって、ぴょんと馬に飛び乗りました。

「一追いして来る。」

　こう言いますと、栄三が馬の口をとらえて、「旦那、それは危のうござんす。」＊　ととめました。

「何を、三人や四人の米どろぼう、お前は後から走って来い。」

　こう言うと、馬の腹を両足で蹴って、道の上に駆け出

24

"Oh, I let some thieves get away. Too bad."

"How far've they gotten away?"

"Uh, over there. You see them with a bag of rice on their shoulders?"

Shielding their eyes from the moonlight with their hands, they gazed in the direction of the village off in the distance.

"Ah, in that case, sir, we can still catch up with them on horseback."

The words were no sooner out than he raced back through the front gate and led out an unsaddled horse.

"Whoa, whoa, whoa!" Calming the spirited horse, Eizō made ready to leap up onto it.

"Wait! Wait! Wait a second!"

Jinshichi tucked up his skirt and slipped the sword he'd been holding in his hand inside his waistband. Then he took the reins from Eizō and, with a leap, mounted the horse.

"I'll give them a chase."

At these words, Eizō grabbed the horse's bit and held the horse in check, saying "Master, it's too dangerous!"

"Don't be silly! Three or four rice thieves? You come running behind."

With this, he kicked the horse's flanks with both feet and raced off down the path through the rice

---

* 危のう ＝ 危ない，ござんす ＝ ございます；compare（お）はようございます．

しました。馬の背中で体をすくめ、前の方をすかすように
して見ているおじいさんの姿は、中々勇ましいもの
だったそうであります。馬は風のように走りました。栄
三も後から一生懸命に駆けました。どろぼうはそのとき
もう隣村の家の陰へ入っていて、影も形も見えませんで
した。

　ところで、おじいさんが隣村へ馬の足音高く駆け込ん
で、そこの村端れへ出ようと、川の橋の近くへやって来
ますと、ちょうど橋の彼方のたもとで休んでいる三人の
男があります。俵のようなものを真ん中に何か話し合っ
ているようです。それでおじいさんはまた大きな声をあ
げました。

「こうらあ、どろぼうめい。」

　しかしどろぼうは少しも逃げようといたしません。ま
るでおじいさんの来るのを待ってるようにじっとしてお
ります。それでおじいさんは、どろぼうがもう動けなく
なったので、おじいさんにお詫びでもするのかと考えま
した。それで馬を少し静かにして、歩かせながら橋を渡っ
て行きました。馬がちょうど橋の真ん中に行ったとき、
おじいさんはどろぼうに、声をかけようといたしました。

　すると、そのときでした。橋の下の水の上にとても大

fields. They say that, hunched down on the horse's back and eyes peering into the distance, old Jinshichi cut quite a heroic figure that night. The horse ran like the wind. And Eizō raced after as fast as he could. The thieves, meanwhile, had gained the other side of the houses in the neighboring village, and neither hide nor hair of them could be seen.

Now, when Jinshichi raced into the village with a great clatter of hoofbeats, intending to come out at its farther edge, and approached a bridge over a river, he spotted three men resting at the foot of the bridge, on the opposite side. They were sitting around something that looked like a bag of rice, and seemed to be carrying on a discussion. Here Jinshichi once again shouted to them:

"So there you are, you thievin' scum!"

But the thieves made not the slightest attempt to run away. As if they had been waiting for the old man to come, they didn't move. Jinshichi thought maybe they couldn't move another step and so were going to apologize to him or something. So he quieted the horse down a bit and started walking it across the bridge. When the horse reached the midpoint of the bridge, Jinshichi started to say something to the thieves.

And that's when it happened. There was this tremendously loud noise over the water under the

きな音が起こりました。そしてしぶきがどっと上に上がって来ました。それで馬がびっくりして、とっとさおを立てたように前足を上げて立ち上がりました。立ち上がったと思うと、それなり、くるりと後ろ向きになり、それから今来た家の方をさして、鉄砲玉のように走り出しました。止めようにも、どうしようにも馬はこうなっては、力に及びません。

「どうどう、どうどう。」

おじいさんは一生懸命手綱を引き引き、何度も何度も叫びつづけました。それを見て、どろぼうたちはハッハッハッハッと腹をかかえて笑いました。

おじいさんの馬はそれでも後ろから来る栄三のところまで駆けて来ると、そこの道に両手をひろげてつったっていた栄三に止められました。

「どうどうどう。」

何度もそう言って、首のところを叩いて、栄三とおじいさんとで、まだ怖れてたじたじする馬をなだめました。それから馬には乗らず二人で両側から手綱を引いて、また橋の方に引き返しました。

「どろぼうの奴、とうとう俵を川の中へ捨てて行ったよ。仕方のない奴だ。置いてくなら道の上へ置いとけばいい

bridge. Then a sudden spray of water rose high into the air. This startled the horse, and it reared up, its front legs raised straight as poles. In practically the same motion it spun round in the opposite direction and shot off like a bullet in the direction of the houses they had just passed. When a horse gets frightened like this, there's nothing anybody can do to control it.

"Whoa, whoa! Whoa, whoa!"

Jinshichi pulled and pulled on the reins as hard as he could and kept shouting at the horse over and over to stop. Watching him, the thieves laughed uproariously, holding their sides.

The horse ran on like this despite all Jinshichi's efforts, till it came to where Eizō was bringing up the rear; there it was stopped by the farmhand, who was standing in the middle of the road with both arms outstretched.

"Whoa, whoa, whoa!"

Repeating this over and over, patting it on the neck, Eizō and Jinshichi managed between the two of them to calm the still frightened and jumpy horse. And then, without getting on, each of them holding one of the reins, they led the horse back towards the bridge.

"Those wretched thieves, in the end they dumped the bag into the river. Useless wretches! If they were going to leave it behind they could've left it on the road."

ものを。」

　二人はそんなことを言い合いながら、橋のところに来て見ますと、もうどろぼうはおりません。川の水も静かになっております。水の中を月の光ですかして見ますと、ちょうど俵のようなものが、その底の方に転がっております。然し何だか少し小さく見えるようで、栄三が竹の棒を拾って来て、上からそれを突っ突いて見ました。コチコチと堅い手ごたえがいたします。

「旦那、こりゃ石ですぜ。」

　栄三が言いますので、おじいさんも突っ突いて見ました。頭の方や胴の方や、どこを突いても堅い石の手ごたえです。

「ほんとうだ。こりゃ、どろぼうに一杯くわされた。」

　そう言って、ふと橋のたもとを見ますと、そこにいつも立っていたお地蔵さまが見えません。

「やっ、これだこれだ。お地蔵さまも御迷惑に。」

　おじいさんも栄三もついおかしくなって笑いました。どろぼうにとうとう旨くだまされた訳であります。それで仕方なく、二人はそこから引き返し、道で二俵の米を拾い、それを馬の背中につけて帰りました。

Exchanging comments like this, they reached the bridge. They saw the thieves were gone. The waters of the river were still again, too. They peered into the water where the moonlight hit it; something that looked like a bag of rice was lying on the bottom. But it looked just a bit too small, somehow, so Eizō fetched a bamboo pole and poked at it from above. It felt hard and solid.

"I say, master, this's a stone!"

Jinshichi's reaction to Eizō's words was to take a few pokes for himself. The top, the middle, no matter where he poked, it felt like hard stone.

"You're right. Man, have I been taken in by those thieves!" As he said this, he happened to glance over to the foot of the bridge. The statue of Jizō that always stood there was gone.

"Aha, so that's it! Even the holy Jizō has been disturbed!"

The ridiculousness of the situation caused both Jinshichi and Eizō to smile. They had been fooled by the thieves with a clever trick. Unable to do anything else now, they retraced their steps, picked up the two bags of rice left along the path, set them on the horse's back, and returned home.

ところで、翌日のことであります。一人の植木屋が板の上に沢山鉢植えの牡丹を載せて、それを担ぎ棒で前後に担いでやって来ました。側にはその親方のような植木屋がついております。その男は襟に芳翠園と書かれたハッピを着ていました。

「へい、今日は、町の香蘭園さんで聞いてまいりました。こちらの旦那様は牡丹が大変お好きだそうでございまして。上方の牡丹商人でございます。今日は珍種、上もの、飛び切りの種類をそろえて持ってまいりました。お買い上げが叶いませんでも、ただ旦那さまの御覧を戴くだけでも結構でございます。」

植木屋は玄関でそう口上を言っておりましたが、庭の開き戸の開いているのを見ると、もうずんずん庭の方へ入ってまいりました。

「おおお、これは結構なお庭だ。おい、きさまもこちらへ入れ。入って、お庭を拝見するがいい。何とあの滝口のこしらえから、築山の雪見燈籠のあたり、何とも言えない眺めじゃないか。石の色といい、松の寂びといい、どうしても庭をこれだけにするのには百年がとこはか

Now, the next day a gardener came along carrying a large number of potted peonies. The pots had been set on a plank suspended front and aft from a shoulder pole. Walking beside the man was a second gardener, who appeared to be the master gardener. He was wearing a tradesman's jacket with the words "Fragrant Green Garden" on his lapel.

"Why, good day to you, sir! I'm here because of what I heard at the 'Aromatic Orchid Garden' in town. They told me the master of this house is very fond of peonies. I am a peony merchant from the Kyoto area. Today I have with me a selection of rare, top-quality, choice varieties. Even if a purchase is not possible, I would be happy just to have the master take a look."

The gardener was delivering this prologue at the front entrance when he noticed that the garden gate was open, whereupon without further ado he marched in.

"My, my, my, this is some garden! Hey you, you come in, too. It'll do you some good to see this garden. Wow, from the way the top of that waterfall is arranged, to the snow-view lantern on the mound, now isn't that an indescribable sight? And the color of the rocks, and the patina on the pine bark, it must take at least a hundred years, for sure, to get a garden to this

かるだろう。」

　親分らしいのは、一人で感心し、一人でしゃべっております。そこへおじいさんが縁側に出て来ました。すると、植木屋はまた何度かお辞儀をして、庭をほめたり、牡丹の効能を言ったり、長々としゃべり立てました。そしておじいさんにはろくろく話もさせないで、庭の踏み石の上や、松の木の根元、岩の陰などに牡丹の鉢を列べました。牡丹はみんなで十鉢ばかりでしたが、その青々とした葉陰から少し色づきかけているつぼみをのぞかせていました。

　植木屋はその一鉢一鉢に就いて、花の美しさからその木の名前などをまた上手にしゃべり立てました。「狂い獅子」というのは乱れ咲きの花で、花びらが房のようにたれるのだというのでした。「濁江の綿」と言いますのは真紅な花で、そのさし渡し五寸からある大輪だと言いました。「雪山」と言うのは、雪のように白いのだそうであります。

　おじいさんはその間ただ「ふん、ふん。」と言うきりで、むつかしい顔をして聞いていました。ほんとうはおじいさんはそれらの牡丹がほしくてならなかったのです。しかし上方から来た商人ですし、それにその牡丹の植わっ

stage!"

The one who was presumably the master gardener was doing all the admiring and all the talking. During his one-man act, old Jinshichi came out onto the verandah. Whereupon the gardener, bowing again and again, once more launched into a long speech, in which he mixed praises for the garden with words about the virtues of peonies. Then, without allowing Jinshichi much chance to say anything, he set out the peony pots on the garden stepping stones, at the base of the pine tree, in the shadow of a rock, and so on. There were ten pots of peonies in all; from between their light bluish-green leaves peeped buds that were ever so slightly beginning to take on color.

The gardener plunged into another smooth monologue describing each and every one of the pots there: the individual names of each of the plants, the beauty of their blossoms, etc., etc., etc. "Crazy Lion," he explained, was so called because the flowers bloomed in jumbled profusion and the petals hung down like tassels. The one called "Zhuo-jiang Brocade" had crimson flowers, large blossoms at least six inches in diameter. "Snowy Mountain" had flowers as white as snow.

During this time the only thing Jinshichi said was "Hmm," "Hmm," as he listened with a grave expression on his face. The truth was, he sorely wanted to have those peonies. But seeing that the merchant had come from the Kyoto area and the pots they were

ている鉢を見るとみなそれがシナ焼の上もので、鉢だけ
でも中々大変な値打ちに思われました。それで値段を聞
いてやめるよりはと思って、植木屋のしゃべるに任せて、
いつまでも黙っていました。

　すると、おしまいになって、とうとう植木屋は自分の
方から値段を言いました。ところが、その値段の安いこ
とと言ったら、それは鉢の値段にも足りない位に思えま
した。おじいさんはそれで直ぐにも、その十鉢全部を買
い取りたいと思いましたけれども、何だか不思議な気が
して考え込みました。牡丹のはやっているときでしたか
ら、そんな値段のある筈がないと思われたのであります。
それで、もしかしたら、これはどこかで盗んで来た牡丹
かも知れない。そんなことがふと考えられたのでありま
す。それでまた買おうと言い兼ねて、ふうん、ふうん、
言いながらしきりに煙草を吸っておりました。おしゃべ
りの植木屋もこれには困ったと見えまして、とうとう少
し腹を立てたような顔になって言いました。

「旦那は牡丹のよしあしがお分かりにならないんじゃあ
ありませんか。これ程の名木を一体どんな値段でお買い
なさろうというのです。菜っ葉や人参とは違いますぜ。」
　そう言うと、腹だたしそうにどんどん鉢を片ずけ、ま

planted in were all top-quality chinaware, he reck-
oned just the pots alone were worth a very consider-
able sum. Therefore, rather than call a halt to the
whole business after asking prices, he figured he'd
just keep quiet and let the gardener talk.

At the end of his spiel, though, the gardener
finally mentioned a price without being asked. Talk
about a low price! Jinshichi figured they wouldn't
cover even the cost of the pots! He was tempted to buy
up the whole lot of ten pots right then and there, but
something about this thing bothered him and gave
him cause to think. Peonies were in popular demand
at the time, so the price shouldn't be that low. Then
the thought suddenly occurred to him that maybe
these peonies were stolen from somewhere. As a result he couldn't bring himself to say he would buy
them, and all he did was puff energetically on his pipe
and say "Hmm," "Hmm."

Even the glib-tongued gardener seemed upset by
this, because finally, a slightly annoyed expression on
his face, he said, "I wonder, sir, if you know good peonies when you see them. What kind of price do you
expect to pay for fine plants like these? It's not as if
they're spinach or carrots, I'll have you know."

With this, he began testily collecting one pot after

た板の上に乗せ始めました。これを見ると、おじいさん
は盗んで来たなどという疑いもなくなり、初めて煙草を
やめて声をかけました。

「まあそう立腹しなさんな。それじゃあ、お前さんの言
い値で、この鉢全部買い取ろう。折角だから置いて行き
なさい。」

　植木屋は愉快そうな声を上げました。

「いや、有り難う存じます。やっぱり旦那は目がおあり
です。いずれ、私もこの花の咲く頃にもう一度まいりま
して、花つくりの秘伝とでもいうようなものを申し上げ
ることに致しましょう。」

　こんな有り様で、植木屋はお金をもらうと喜んで帰っ
て行きました。

　ところが、それから四五日して、牡丹の花が美しく開
き始めた朝のことでした。おじいさんが屋敷の中を見
廻っておりますと、米倉の前に短冊が一枚落ちていまし
た。それにはこんなことが書いてあります。

another and setting them back on the plank. When Jinshichi saw him doing this, his suspicions about their being stolen and the like vanished, and he stopped smoking and finally spoke up.

"Now, now, don't get so excited. All right, I'll buy all your pots at the price you named. Since you've gone to the trouble, you can leave them where they are."

The gardener's tone of voice was now one of glee. "Why, thank you very much! You do have a discriminating eye after all, sir. I'll tell you what, in a few days, when these flowers are coming into bloom, I'll come once again and I'll pass on to you what you might call the secret of cultivating flowers."

In this fashion, the gardener received his money and returned on his way a happy man.

Now, four or five days later the peony buds began opening into beautiful blossoms. It was early in the morning, and Jinshichi was making a tour of inspection of the grounds, when he found a strip of fancy paper, of the kind used for writing tanka or haiku on, lying on the ground in front of the rice shed. On it were written the following words:

「花の秘伝、何事も用心第一、用心第一、あした嵐の吹

かぬものかは。」

　おじいさんが不思議そうにしてこれを見ていますと、

外から門内に駆け込んで来たものがありました。

「旦那旦那、米倉が空ですぜ。」

　栄三がうろたえて呼んでおりました。

　昨夜の間に、どろぼうは米倉の外側を流れている川に

一そうの船を引いて来て、倉の壁を切り破り、そこから

五十俵もの米を盗んでしまったのでした。さて、その夜

のことおじいさんの子に、松山お米、即ち善太のおばあ

さんが生まれました。お米を取られたというので、こん

な名をつけたのだそうであります。

The secret of flowers:
In all things vigilance,
Vigilance first and foremost;
You never know when a storm
Might blow on the morrow!

As Jinshichi stood puzzling over the words, someone came running in through the front gate.

"Master, master! The rice shed is empty!" It was Eizō, calling out in much confusion.

During the night thieves had towed a boat down the stream that flowed along past the outer side of the rice shed, had broken through the wall of the shed, and had removed all of fifty bags of rice. Well, that night a child was born to Jinshichi: Zenta's grandmother, Matsuyama O-Yone. And so the reason he gave her that name, the story goes, is because his *o-kome* had been stolen.

Grandfather's Hobbyhorse

TSUBOTA Jōji

お馬

　もと庄屋をしていたお祖父さんは、その頃でもまだ頭に髷を結っていました。断髪令と言って、髷を切って、今頃のみんなの頭のようにせよという規則が出来てから、十年も立っておりましたが、お祖父さんは昔のままの髷を頭の上に乗っけて、それを自慢にしていました。

　お祖父さんは一風変った咳をしました。

「えっへえんー。」

　とても物々しい咳き方なのですが、これがまた自慢の一つでした。でも、えへんはいいのですが、くしゃみと来たら、村中へ響くような大きなものでした。

「はっくしょうんーん。」

　初めは普通なのですが、終の「ん」を長く引張って、もう一つ「ん」をつけ加えるようなくしゃみでした。この咳き方や、くしゃみの仕方で、ライオンが一声で狐や兎をふるえさすように村のものみんなを恐れさせると思っていたのでありましょう。

　お祖父さんは槍や刀が好きでした。床の間にはいつも

44

Grandfather's Hobbyhorse

He once had been a village headman, so Grandfather still did his hair up in a topknot, even in those days. Ten years had passed since the regulation had come down ordering everybody to have their hair cut the way people have it cut nowadays, but Grandfather still had his hair knotted on top of his head, just like in the old days, and he was very proud of it.

Grandfather had his own special way of coughing. "Her-hem!" It was a very show-offish way of coughing. This was another thing Grandfather was proud of.

Still, his cough wasn't so bad compared to his sneeze. When he sneezed, it was so loud it would reverberate round the whole village. "Ah-choooo-oo!" It started off like an ordinary sneeze, but he would drag out the -oo ending, and tack another -oo onto that. He probably thought that this way of coughing and sneezing made everyone in the village afraid of him, the same way a lion lets out a roar and sets the foxes and rabbits atrembling.

Grandfather was fond of the spear and the sword.

鎧甲が飾ってありました。そしてその側に、鹿の角の刀かけに刀が大小二振のせてありました。長押には槍、長刀*、弓などがかけてありました。その下には昔の和鞍と言う、侍の使った鞍が台に乗せて飾ってありました。

その中に座って、お祖父さんは煙草を吸っては、お茶を飲んでいました。そしてその合間合間に槍や刀の手入れをしていました。お祖父さんは刀を磨くのがとても上手で、またその効能を言うことも大変なものでした。お祖父さんは煙草を煙管で飲みました。煙管で灰吹きを叩く音がまた中々ぎょうぎょうしいものでした。その叩き方でお祖父さんのその日の機嫌が分かるとみんなは言っていました。

お祖父さんが怒ると、それは大変でした。怒ることはめずらしく、一年に一度か二度のことでしたが、怒ったとなると、きちんと座って、側にちゃんと刀を置いていました。これまでまだ一度もそれを抜いたことはないのですが、それには誰でもまいってしまいました。あるとき、町から来た屋根職人が、酔ぱらって、お祖父さんの前へ出ました。そして、お祖父さんのやかましいことを知らないで、つい失礼なことを言いました。すると、お祖父さんは、「無礼ものッ。」と大声でどなって、直ぐ

46

He always had a suit of armor and a helmet set out in the living room alcove. Next to them, on a sword rack made from deer antlers, were placed a pair of swords, one long and one short. On the crossbeam hung spear, halberd, and bow and arrows. Below these was an old-fashioned "Japanese saddle," as it was called, the kind of saddle used by samurai; this was ornamentally arranged on a table.

Grandfather would sit in the middle of all his gear and have a smoke and sip tea. Between smokes and sips he would work on a spear or a sword. He was very good at polishing swords, and the effect of his labor was something spectacular.

He used a long-stemmed pipe when he smoked. The noise he made when tapping the ashes out of his pipe was, again, produced with great flamboyance. Everyone said that you could tell what mood Grandfather was in by the way he tapped his pipe.

When he got angry, watch out! He rarely did get angry, maybe once or twice a year, but when he did, he would sit bolt upright, the sword ready at his side. To this day he has never once unsheathed it, but just its presence was enough to daunt anyone. One time, a roofer from town who'd had too much to drink went into the house to talk to Grandfather. Not knowing what a stickler Grandfather was for proper manners, the man happened to say something that wasn't proper. Grandfather's reaction was to roar at the man: "Insolent boor!" and to rise at once to one knee and

立膝になり、側の刀を取り上げました。職人はびっくりして、わっと言って逃げていきました。だからもう、刀を側に置いている前へ呼び付けられるとなったら、誰でも始めから両手をついて丁寧にお詫びをしました。

お祖父さんには仲のいい友だちが一人ありました。それがまたおなじように頭に髷を残していました。その人はその頃馬の先生をしていました。もっとも馬の稽古をする人は他に誰もなくて、ただお祖父さんばかりの先生でした。それでも昔は殿様の馬の先生だったそうであります。

その人は月に何回か、お祖父さんのところへやって来ました。お祖父さんは馬を三頭も持っていました。それでその日になると、作男が二頭の馬をつなぐものへつなぎました。それは今頃の器械体操の金棒のような形をしていて、両側の柱に環がついていました。その環へ馬の手綱を結びました。馬には金銀の模様のついた和風の馬具を乗せました。鐙などは昔の絵にある佐々木高綱や梶原景季の使ったものと同じかっこうでした。＊

その馬へお祖父さんと馬の先生とが羽織袴で乗りま

pick up the sword at his side. The roofer let out a howl of terror and ran off. After that, if anyone was called in to see him and he had the sword at his side, the man always made sure he first bowed politely with both hands to the floor and apologized for interrupting.

Grandfather had one very close friend. This friend, too, kept the topknot on his head, the same as Grandfather. In those days he used to teach horse riding. There was nobody else besides Grandfather who took lessons, though, so really Grandfather was his only pupil. But in the old days, it was said, he had taught riding to the lord of that province.

He came several times a month to visit Grandfather. Grandfather had three horses. So on those days when the riding master came, one of the farmhands would tether two of the horses to the hitching rail. This hitching rail was shaped something like the gymnastic bars you see nowadays, only it had rings attached to each of the upright posts. The horses' reins were tied to these rings. Then on each horse the farmhand put Japanese-style trappings with gold and silver decorations. The stirrups and other gear looked like what the famous warriors Sasaki Takatsuna and Kajiwara Kagesue used, as shown in old paintings.

Grandfather and the riding master, both in full riding dress, mounted these horses. In their hands

* These two warriors of the late twelfth century are famous because of the story that they raced their steeds across the Uji River because each wanted to be the first to fight the enemy camped on the other side (the year was 1184).

49

した。手には竹の根で作った鞭をにぎっていました。

　お祖父さんの屋敷の周囲へは広い道が造ってありました。そこを馬場に使っていたのです。道の両側には松が植っていました。その間を二人の老人がぱっぱっぱっぱっと馬に乗って走りました。ぱっぱっというのは普通の馬の歩き方ではありません。馬に右の前後、左の前後と、片側の両足を一度に上げさせて歩かす歩き方です。これは昔、儀式のときに、殿様の前などでやった乗り方なのでしょうか。こうして乗ると、胸がい、しりがいなどという馬具の飾りがひらひらゆれ、くつわがしゃんしゃんと、にぎやかな音を立てました。すると、馬の先生は根鞭で鞍下の革具を打ってはげしい音を立てました。ときには、はいよう、はいようと、とてもすごいかけ声をかけました。

　村の子供たちはそんなときいつでも道の両側の松の木にのぼって、枝に鈴なりになって見物しました。それは、こんな二人の侍が馬に乗るのが面白いばかりではありません。お祖父さんは人が見物するのがとても好きでした。馬乗りがすむと、見物していた子供たちにおせんべいを幾枚かずつくれるのがきまりでした。

　「おお、よく見てくれたなぁ。また来て見てくれるんだ

they held whips made from bamboo roots.

There was a wide trail made around the perimeter of Grandfather's property. They used the trail as a riding ground. On both sides of the trail were planted pine trees. The two old men would make their horses go pacing between these rows of pine trees. Now, pacing is not a horse's ordinary way of walking. It consists of having a horse walk by moving both legs on the same side together: the front and hind right legs, then the front and hind left legs, and so on. Perhaps this was the way horses they rode horses in the presence of the lord of the province during formal ceremonies in the old days. When they rode this way, the martingales and cruppers would flap rhythmically and the bits would make a jingle-jingle sound. Then the riding master would beat the whip against the leather under the saddle and raise a fierce clatter. Every now and then he let out a tremendous shout: "High-oh!"

The children in the village would always climb into the pine trees along the trail on these days and watch in small clusters from the branches. It wasn't only because they found the horse riding of such a pair of "samurai" amusing. Grandfather was very glad to have onlookers. It was a custom of his that, when the riding was over, he always gave the children who'd been watching a few rice crackers apiece.

"Oh, nice of you to come and watch. Come and

ぞ。」と、お祖父さんはとてもいい機嫌です。

　お祖父さんの馬好きは五里も十里も遠くまで有名でした。馬の甚七さんと言えば、大人はだれでも知っていました。

　お祖父さんは若い頃は特にお酒が好きでした。酔っぱらうと、冬でも夏でも真裸になりました。そしてふんどし一つに刀を一本さしこみました。それで鞍も置かない裸の馬に乗りました。そんなときは馬場などでなく、村の道を乗り廻しました。そして、「若いときからお馬にめして、手綱さばきのほどのよさ。」と、こんな歌を謡いました。あるとき、それは明治の前で、侍が刀をさして、道を歩いている頃のことだったそうです。お祖父さんは酔っぱらって、この裸の馬乗りをやっていました。春のことでしたが、お祖父さんが馬に乗っていく道の彼方に、一人の人が草の上に寝ころんでいました。

　お祖父さんは、それも酒に酔って寝ているのだろう、ぐらいに考えて、駆けていきました。側を通り過ぎるとき、よく見ると、それはどこかの侍でした。お祖父さんも名字帯刀を許されている庄屋の子でしたけれども、相手が侍ならば、馬から下りて、お辞儀をして通らなければなりません。しかしその侍は眠っているらしいし、馬

52

watch again, now, eh?" Grandfather would be in a very good mood.

Grandfather's love of riding was known to everybody for miles and miles around. Just mention "Horserider Jinshichi" and any grown-up knew whom you were talking about.

When he was young, Grandfather liked to drink sake. When he got drunk, winter or summer, he would strip naked and slip a sword into his loincloth. He wouldn't bother to saddle his horse but would ride bareback. At such times he didn't use the riding ground or the like; he rode up and down the roads of the village. And then he'd sing this song: "Been ridin' horses since his youth, how well he holds the reins."

They tell the story of how one time — this was before the Meiji Restoration, when samurai still walked the streets with swords at their sides — Grandfather got drunk and was doing his bareback riding. It was springtime, and up ahead along the road that Grandfather was taking somebody was lying on the grass.

Grandfather didn't give the matter much thought — "Just another fellow who's had too much to drink and is sleeping it off" — and kept on riding. As he passed he took a better look: it was some samurai he'd never seen before. Now, Grandfather was the son of a village headman and he too was entitled to use a last name and wear swords, but if he met a samurai he was obliged to get off his horse and bow before passing. But the samurai seemed to be asleep, for one thing, and the horse was galloping along, for another,

は駆け足でかけているのですから、えい、かまうものか
と思って、そのまま通り過ぎました。通り過ぎたかと思
うと、後で大きな声がしました。

「こら、待てッ。」

　後を振り向くと、侍は起き上がって、刀の柄に手をか
けていました。お祖父さんは困ったことになったと思い
ましたが、馬は駆けつづけているので、ちぇッ、逃げろ
と思って、侍が大きな声でどなるのを、聞こえないふり
をして競馬のように馬を走らせて逃げてしまいました。

　それから遠廻りをして家へ帰り、馬を厩に入れ、くつ
わを納屋に置こうとして、納屋に入りますと、後でまた
さっきの侍の声がしました。有名な馬の甚七のことです
から、逃げても侍は家を知っていました。そこで大変な
勢いで追っかけて来たのでした。侍はもうそのときには
刀を抜き放していました。

　これを見ると、お祖父さんはその納屋の大きな戸を内
からごろごろっと締めてしまいました。すると、追っか
けて来た侍は目の前で戸がしまったので、その戸を蹴っ
たり叩いたりしました。しかし大きな戸ですからびくと
もしません。侍は、しまいには気狂いのように怒りたけっ
て、＊　何をというなり持っている刀をその戸の板へ

54

so Grandfather thought, "Heck, what difference does it make?" and went by without stopping. But no sooner had he passed than he heard a shout from behind.

"Hey, you! Stop!"

Grandfather looked back, to see the samurai standing with his hand on the hilt of his sword. Grandfather figured he was in real trouble now, but since the horse was still galloping, he thought, "What the heck, let's make a run for it," and, pretending he didn't hear the samurai's shouts, he raced the horse at top speed and hightailed it out of there.

He returned home via a long detour, put the horse in its stable, and had just entered the barn to put the bridle away when from behind he heard the samurai's voice again. "Horserider Jinshichi" was so famous, you see, that even though he'd run away the samurai knew where to find him. Thus the samurai had come at full speed in pursuit of Grandfather. And here the samurai was now, his sword already out of its scabbard.

When Grandfather saw this, he rolled the heavy, rumbling door of the barn shut from the inside. The door closed just in front of the pursuing samurai. He kicked it and pounded on it. But it was big and heavy, and didn't budge a bit. In the end the samurai fumed and raged like a madman. "You so-an'-so!" he said, as he plunged the sword in his hand into a panel of the door.

* The word 怒り can also be pronounced おこり, but in this combination the pronunciation given is more common.

ぐっと突きさしました。

「こらっ、これでも開けんかッ。」

　侍はそう言って、刀を根元までつッこんで切尖を上げ下げして、どなりたてました。するとお祖父さんは持っていたくつわをその刀の先に引っかけ、その上へ手綱をぐるぐる巻にしました。そして、そこにあった大きな杵で刀を上から二三度打ち下ろしました。刀は戸の厚い横木に喰い入って、外から引っ張っても、めったに動かないようになってしまいました。

　そうしておいて、お祖父さんはその納屋の別の戸口をそっと開いて、侍から見えない、壁の方へ出て来ました。そこから顔を覗けてうかがうと、侍はぶつぶつひとりごとを言いながら、一生けんめいにその刀を引き抜こうとしています。その間にお祖父さんはしのび足で、そこを逃げだし、裸のまま村のお医者さんのところへ駆けつけました。

　このお医者さんはその頃有名な長崎帰りの洋医で、殿様の病気も診る御典医というのでした。その人に侍への仲裁を頼んだのです。お医者さんは直ぐに家来をつれてやって来ました。家来と言っても侍で、刀を二本さしていました。お祖父さんも刀をさして、お医者さんの家来

"I'll show you! *Now* you gonna open up?" he said, and he shoved the sword in right to the hilt, then moved the point of it up and down as he stormed loudly. What Grandfather did then was, he hooked the bit in his hands over the tip of the sword and wound the reins round and round it. Then he used a big wooden pestle that was near the door to give the sword a few blows on top and thus drive it farther down into the wood. The sword blade bit into the thicker crosspiece in the door, with the result that it scarcely moved at all when pulled from the outside.

This done, Grandfather quietly opened another door of the barn and slipped out on the wall side, where the samurai couldn't see him. He peeped around the corner of the barn: there was the samurai, muttering curses and trying might and main to pull the sword out of the door. While he was struggling with the sword, Grandfather made a getaway on tiptoe. Dressed only in his loincloth, he ran to the house of the village doctor.

This doctor was a famous doctor of Western medicine who had studied in Nagasaki, and he was official doctor to the lord of the province as well. Grandfather asked him to act as peacemaker with the samurai. The doctor went at once to Grandfather's house, accompanied by his retainers. Though I say "retainers," they were still samurai, with two swords in their belts. Grandfather also wore a sword and went along at the doctor's side as one of his retainers.

のように側についていきました。

「あなたはどなたですか。私は典医、山川平九郎ですが。」

　まだ刀を抜こうと焦っている侍にお医者さんは呼びかけました。これを聞くと、侍は顔色を変えました。

「いや、これはこれは、少し酒興が過ぎましてな、とんだところをお目にかけました。」

　これでもう訳なく仲裁がすみました。お祖父さんは知らぬ顔をして、戸を開けたり、刀をとってやったりしました。

　この侍がつけた刀の跡が明治になっても、はっきり戸の板に残っていました。これがまたお祖父さん自慢の一つで、いつ頃かいたものか、その刀傷の側に、筆で、こうかきつけてありました。

「嘉永参年参月廿日、甚七遭難の跡。」

　でも、お祖父さんは誰に聞かれても、くわしい話はしませんでした。ただ、人にその跡が見えるように、いつも戸をしめて置くことや、その側を通るときのお祖父さんのいかめしい様子などで、みんなが、お祖父さんの得意さを察するだけでした。

"Please identify yourself. I am Yamakawa Heikurō, official doctor to the lord."

This is how the doctor identified himself to the samurai, who was still tugging frantically at his sword. When the samurai heard who the speaker was, his face changed color.

"Er, sorry about this . . . a bit too much carousing, I guess. I am afraid I have made a spectacle of myself."

After this, the peacemaking was completed without any trouble. Grandfather kept a straight face as he opened the barn door and took the sword out for the samurai.

Even in the Meiji Period the gash made by this samurai's sword remained clearly visible in the wood of the door. It was another of the things Grandfather was proud of. It's not known exactly when he wrote it, but next to the sword mark were written, in black ink, the words:

"20 March 1850. Vestige of Jinshichi's close call"

Yet no matter who asked him about the incident, Grandfather never said much about it. They all could guess how proud he was of it, though, from the fact that he kept the barn door shut so people could see the gash, and from the majestic bearing with which he always passed in front of it.

　日清戦争の終り頃、お祖父さんのただ一人の友だちの、馬の先生が亡くなりました。先生には騎兵中尉になる一人息子がありましたが、これが戦争で死にました。すると、間もなく先生も病気になって死にました。先生は親一人、子一人だったのです。それで先生が死んでしまえば、お墓を建てる人さえありません。

　お祖父さんはそれを大変気の毒に思って、先生が死ぬと、自分の髷を切り取って、それを先生と一しょに墓に埋めました。墓も騎兵中尉のと一しょにお祖父さんが建てました。墓には漢文で、お祖父さんと仲がよくて、一しょに馬に乗って遊んだということを彫らせました。

　馬の先生が亡くなり、頭の髷を切り落とすとお祖父さんはすっかり年をとって、もう馬にも乗れなくなりました。それでお祖父さんは考えた末、屋敷の隅に小屋を建て、その中へ木馬を造らせてすえつけました。その背中の上には昔の鞍を置きました。そしてお祖父さんは羽織袴でそれに乗り、根鞭を叩いて、掛声をかけました。

「はいよう。はいよう。」

　馬の首が動くようになっていましたので、

60

Just about the end of the Sino-Japanese War Grandfather's only friend, the riding master, died. The master had an only son who had been a Cavalry First Lieutenant, but he'd died during the war. Soon afterwards the master also took sick and died. Theirs had been a one-parent, one-child family. As a result, when the master died there wasn't anyone to erect a tombstone for him.

Grandfather felt terribly sorry about this, and when the master died Grandfather cut off his own topknot and buried it in the grave along with the master. He then erected a tombstone for the master alongside that of the Cavalry First Lieutenant. On the tombstone he had a stonecutter carve, in classical Chinese, that the master had been Grandfather's close friend and that they had enjoyed riding together.

After the riding master died and he had cut off his own topknot, Grandfather aged rapidly. He no longer had the strength to ride a horse. Still, after some thought, he had a shed built in one corner of his property, and in it he had a custom-made wooden horse set up. On its back he placed a saddle of the kind they used in the old days. Then Grandfather would mount it in full riding dress. Beating it with the bamboo-root whip, he would urge it on with a "High-oh! High-oh!"

The horse was made so that its neck could move.

「どうどう。どうどう。」

　そんなことを言って、手綱を引っぱりました。その度に木の首ががっちゃんがっちゃんと言いました。でも、生きた馬に乗っていたときより、この木馬のときの方が不思議とお祖父さんは勇しく見えました。鞭を絶えず馬具の上で鳴らして、すごい掛声で、どなりました。

　そのうちにお祖父さんの体は鞍の上で躍り上がりはね上がりました。じっとしている木馬なのに、これは不思議なことでした。あるときなど、お祖父さんはその木馬から落ちまでしました。これは稽古があまり激しかったせいかも知れません。

　お祖父さんはそうした稽古を、子供たちに見られるのをきらいました。小屋にはちゃんと戸をしめ、戸にはちゃんと内から錠を下ろしました。ところが、子供の方では生きた馬より、ずっとずっとこの方が好きで、お祖父さんの掛声を聞くと、小屋の戸口にたかって、節穴や、板の隙間からのぞきました。そしてにッと滑稽な顔をし合ったり、くすくすとしのび笑いをしたりしました。

　お祖父さんが稽古を終り、内から戸の錠をはずしかけると、子供らはぞろぞろつながって、納屋や倉の間のようなところへ隠れていき、お祖父さんが、汗だくだくに

"Whoa! Whoa!" Grandfather would say, pulling on the reins. Every time he did this, the wooden neck went *click-clack*, *click-clack*. Strangely enough, Grandfather cut a more gallant figure when he was on this wooden horse than when he rode a real horse. He would beat the whip against the trappings non-stop and urge it on with tremendous shouts.

Before long Grandfather's body would be bouncing up and down on the saddle. Considering it was a wooden horse that didn't move, this was something quite remarkable. Every so often Grandfather actually fell from the wooden horse. No doubt from the exercise getting too violent.

Grandfather did not like having these exercises of his seen by the children. He always made sure the door of the shed was closed fast and then barred. As far as the children were concerned, however, this was far, far more fun than the rides on the live horses, and as soon as they heard Grandfather's shouts they would flock to the door of the shed and peek in through knotholes and cracks between boards. Then they would exchange amused looks and stifle their giggles and sniggers.

When Grandfather finished his exercises and walked over to unbar the door, the children scattered in little groups and hid between the barn and the storage shed and similar places, and then when Grandfather, dripping sweat, entered the house, they'd all

なって家の中へ入ると、またそこから出て来ました。そして、みんなで、こっそり戸をあけて鼠のように中へもぐりこみ、馬の背中へ、一度に五人も六人もかたまって跨がりました。一とうまえの子は、おし出されて、首に抱きつきます。一とうあとの一人は後へすべり落ちそうになるので、後向きになって、尻のところを両手でつかんだりしていました。

始めの内はみんなは声を立てないようにして、手綱だけを引いて、首をぎっこんばったんと動かすばかりでしたが、そのうちには、いつでも喧嘩を始めました。何にしても手綱を引っ張るのが一番面白いので、僕が持つ、僕に持たせろ、と争い始めるのです。

みんなは、かわるがわる少しの間ずつしか持てないので、自然引っ張り方が荒っぽくなり、しまいには「はいよう一。」などと、お祖父さんの掛声を真似るものさえ出て来ました。

すると、木馬に乗れないでいる一人が節穴から外を見て、そらっ、お祖父さんだ、とおどかします。みんなはばらばらと木馬から下りて、その腹の下に縮こまってしゃがみ、声を殺していました。でも木馬の腹を下からみると、中がらんどうで、何だか滑稽なのでそのまま

come out of hiding. In a body they'd go and quietly open the shed door and crawl inside like so many little mice. Then they'd sit astride the horse's back in groups of five or six at a time. The one farthest up front would be pushed out of the saddle and had to cling tightly to the neck; the one farthest back would almost be sliding off, so he'd have to face backwards and hold onto the back end of the horse with both hands.

At first they would be careful not to raise their voices, so they would only pull on the reins and rock the head back and forth, but it never took long before a quarrel started. The reason was simple: since pulling on the reins was the most fun, a fight always began over who was going to hold them. "*I'll* hold them." "Let *me* hold them!" "No, *I* wanna hold 'em!"

With all of them taking turns they could each hold the reins for only a short while, so inevitably the rein-pulling would get rougher and rougher, until in the end you'd have some of them shouting "High-oh!" and the like, imitating Grandfather's cries.

About this point, one of the children who hadn't managed to get a ride on the horse would be looking out through a knothole and suddenly scare everybody by saying in a loud whisper, "Psst, the old man's coming!" There'd be a mad scramble off the wooden horse and they'd all squat in a huddle under its belly, stifling their voices. But then they'd look up at the horse's belly and see it was all hollow, and this would

また、そこで遊び始めるのでした。

　お祖父さんはこんなときには、子供らが馬具をこわすのを心配して、座敷の方で、「えへーん」「えへーん」と言いました。でも、しまいには負けて、子供たちが小屋の中へはいっても、だまっていました。それからつぎには自分で子供らのところへやって来て、馬の乗り方を教えたりするようになりました。自分でも乗って子供に見せました。

　お祖父さんの部屋の側にある松の木に鳩が巣を造ったことがありました。お祖父さんはこれをとても喜びました。折々縁側へ出て木の上を舞うている大きな鳥を眺めていました。

　ところが、ふとその頃から病気になりました。そして子供らが木馬で騒ぐ声を聞きながら、鳩の子がまだ巣立たないうちに亡くなってしまいました。お祖父さんの葬式には馬が三頭、昔風の美しい鞍をおいて、お供をしました。

strike them as amusing and they'd start playing inside it.

At this stage Grandfather would begin to worry that the children might do some damage to the horse or gear, so from his front room he would give his famous cough: "Her-hem, her-hem!" In the end he gave in, though, and he didn't say anything when the children were inside the shed. The next stage after that was when he started going himself to join the children and would teach them how to ride the horse. He'd even get on the wooden horse himself to demonstrate to them.

Some pigeons made their nest in the pine tree next to Grandfather's room. Grandfather was overjoyed at this. Time and again he'd step out onto the verandah and watch the big birds circling over the tree.

It was round about that time, though, that Grandfather suddenly took sick. And with the shouts of the children noisily playing with the wooden horse ringing in his ears, with the pigeon chicks still too small to leave the nest, Grandfather passed away. At his funeral, his casket was accompanied by three horses decked out in the beautiful saddles of olden days.

Dreams

TSUBOTA Jōji

ゆ　め

　ぼくはゆめを見た。おもしろかったよ。

「おれは（あ）の字だ。」

　そういう声がしたので、見ると、暗い中に電灯が付いていたように、（あ）という字がパッとうつっていた。

「あ、あの（あ）の字か。」

　ぼくは思った。すると、その（あ）の字がクルクル舞いだした。マイマイツブロという虫が舞うだろう。あんなにクルクル、そうだ、8の字や、3の字や、2の字を、いくつもつないだように舞うのだ。すると、どうだ。このへんにたくさんいろいろな字がちらばっていたと見え、その一つとくっついて、たちまち「あさ」という字ができてしまった。

「あさ、ああ、あの朝か。」

　ぼくはそう思った。しかし「あさ」はまだクルクル舞いを止めず、8の字や、3の字を何回かやった。と、後に（ひ）の字がくっついて、それは「あさひ」となってしまった。

70

Dreams

I had a dream. An interesting one.

"I'm the letter A," said a voice, and when I looked, the letter A flashed before me, as if a light went on in the middle of darkness.

"Ah, the letter A, huh?" I thought. Just then the letter A began spinning. A snail shell goes round and round, right? That's how it went round — as if it were doing several figure eights and threes and twos, one right after the other. Then you know what? There must've been a lot of syllables lying scattered about nearby, because it stuck onto one of them and straightaway the word ASA was made.

"ASA? Oh, that must be the *asa* meaning 'morning'," I thought. But now ASA wouldn't stop spinning round, and it did several figure eights and threes. Then the syllable HI stuck onto it, and it became ASAHI.

「なるほど、朝日の（ひ）だな。ふーん、これはきっと、新しいゆうぎなんだぞ。」

　そう思った時、（あ）の字はまた一字だけはなれて、クルクル舞いをやり、今度は、（た）の字を後にくっつけた。それから何回も、（た）の字を後にひきずって回り回っていたが、なかなか、次の字が見つからないらしく、あっちへ行って舞ったり、こっちへいって止まったりした。ぼくは、

「あた、あた。」

と口のうちで言ってみた。そして、

「あたん、あたんじゃないかな。」

とも考えた。

「もしかしたら、暖かかも知れないな。」

　そう思った。とたんに、（あた）の次に（ま）の字がくっついた。

「なあんだ。あたまか。」

　ついまた、ぼくは口のうちで言ってしまった。すると、（あ）の字は（た）の字と（ま）の字をどこかへやってしまって、一字だけ舞い始めた。今度は、どんな字とくっつくか。いよいよおもしろくなって、（あ）の字のクルクル舞いを見つめていた。

"Why, of course, the HI of *asahi*, 'morning sun'! Aha, I'll bet this is some new kind of game!"

Just as I was thinking this, the letter A separated from the rest and went into its spinning dance again. This time it stuck onto the syllable TA. Then it went round and round several times, dragging the TA behind it; it seemed to have trouble finding the next syllable, because it kept on going off and spinning around, then coming back and stopping.

I repeated to myself the syllables ATA . . . , ATA . . . . Then I thought, "ATAN, it couldn't be *atan*, 'wood coal,' could it? Or maybe *atataka*, 'warm'?" The thought no sooner crossed my mind than the syllable MA stuck onto ATA.

"Of all things! *Atama*, 'head'!" Again I automatically said the word to myself. But then the letter A got rid of the TA and the MA somewhere and began spinning by itself. Now what syllables will it stick onto, I wonder? This was getting more interesting by the minute. I watched the letter A do its whirling dance.

「あし。」

　今度は（あし）という字で止まってしまった。ぼくは
おもしろくなかった。アワビだの、アカハタだの、アユ
だの、アンパンだの、いろいろ考えていたのに、一つも
当たらなかった。それに、（あし）なんて、けちな言葉な
んで、めんどうくさくなって、

「もう、こんな物見ないで、眠ってしまおう。」
と考えた。

　それから少し眠ったような気がした。すると、暗い中
に一本の足が出てきた。

　その時ぼくは思った。

「これは、さっきのつづきなんだな。」

　ところが、その足が、足と言っても、人間の足ではな
い。電信柱のような物だった。しかも、その上に頭が付
いていた。それも人間や馬や牛の頭ではない。何か台の
ような物だった。しかし、ぼくには、

「あれが頭なんだな。」

とすぐ分かった。すると、その頭の上に、いつのまに
か太陽が出てのっかってた。真っ赤な、まるい太陽だ。
あさひなんだ。まぶしいくらい光る。とても暖かい。

　ぼくはまた考えた。

ASHI.

This time it stopped with just the two syllables: ASHI. I didn't find *that* very interesting. I had been thinking of things like *awabi* 'abalone,' *akahata* 'Red Flag,' *ayu* 'sweetfish,' or *ampan* 'bean-jam bun,' but I guessed wrong on all of them. To top it off, *ashi*, 'leg,' was such a plain word. I decided it wasn't worth the effort.

"Let's stop watching this stuff and get some sleep," I thought.

I had the feeling I slept a while after that. Then a leg appeared in the middle of the darkness. I thought to myself, "This is a continuation of before."

But while the leg was a leg, it wasn't a human leg. It was more like a telephone pole. And there was a head attached to the top. It wasn't a man's or a horse's or a cow's head, either. It was more flat, like a desk or something. Still, I knew right away that it was a head. Then suddenly the sun came out and rested on top of the head. It was a bright-red, round sun. The morning sun. It shone with almost blinding light. And it was very warm.

I had another idea.

「よく太陽をかんさつしておこう。」

　で、まず、太陽とぼくとの間のきょりを目そくではかった。二百メートルくらいあった。それから、太陽の形とその大きさを見た。それは、まんまるいすいかのような形で、大きさはちょっけい二十センチはあったろう。そのおもさは分からなかった。しかし、ぼくは、

「あれは、なまりと同じくらいのおもさだ。」

　と思った。だって、そのスイカのような太陽は、ドロドロにとけている金ぞくから出来ているように思えたからだ。ほのおのような物は見えなかった。ひょうめんはやわらかくて、ブヨブヨしているようだった。温度は？それは分からなかった。でも、ずいぶん暖かだったよ。とにかく、こんなに近く太陽を見た者は、今までだれ一人なかったのだから、ぼくは、よくおぼえておこうと考えた。

　それからぼくは眠ったのか、少しは目がさめていたのか知らないけれど、はっきり目がさめてみたら、もう朝だった。それでも、はっきりその太陽を思い出すことができた。今でも思い出すことができる。そこで、

「ぼくは太陽を見た。」

　だれかに言いたくてならなかったけれど、ぼくは言わ

"I'll take a close look at the sun."

So the first thing I did was take an eye measurement of the distance between me and the sun. There was about 200 meters between us. Next I looked at the shape and the size of the sun. It was like a perfectly round watermelon in shape, and it had, oh, I'd say a diameter of at least twenty centimeters. Its weight? That I couldn't tell. But I thought, "It weighs about the same as lead." This is because it looked to me as if that watermelon-like sun was made from some mushy molten metal. I didn't see anything like flames. The surface looked soft and spongy. The temperature? That I didn't know. But it was quite warm, let me tell you. Anyway, since nobody's ever seen the sun from so close before, I decided to take careful note of everything.

Whether I slept after that or was only dozing, I don't know, but when I woke up for good it was already morning. Even so I could still recall that sun clearly. I can recall it even now.

Anyway, I was dying to tell someone I'd seen the

なかった。そんな事を言うと、みんな笑うに決まっているからだ。だがそう考えてみると、ゆめの、あの太陽は、もしかしたら人工太陽かも知れない。そして、もう世界のどこかで作られているかも知れない。作られていなくても、だれかが、発明して、トウキョウやオオサカに、取り付けるだろう。そうしたら、電灯やすみがなくても、ぼくたちは少しも困らない。

　そうだ、だれも発明する人がなかったら、ぼくが発明する。そして、電気とすみに困っていらっしゃるおかあさんをよろこばせてあげる。おかあさんばかりではない。世の中の人がどんなによろこぶか知れない。

　よし、ぼくは勉強して、人工太陽を発明する。

　ところで、ぼくはまたゆめを見た。今度はこわいゆめだった。

　ある晩のこと、気が付いてみたら、ぼくは学校の教室の中にいた。先生はいらっしゃらなかったが、田中くんや伊藤くんや川上くんや、みんながいるようだった。かってに話をしているので、教室の中はガヤガヤしていた。その時、外から、ドッド、ドッドというあらあらしい足音が聞こえた。みだれた足音だった。ぼくは大急ぎで、窓の所へ行ってみた。みんなも窓のそばにかけよった。

sun, but I didn't tell anyone. If I told people what I'd seen they'd all laugh at me for sure, that's why. But now that I think about it, maybe that sun in my dream is a man-made, artificial sun. And maybe somewhere in the world they're already making it. Even if it's not being made at present, someone will invent it, and then they'll install it in places like Tokyo and Osaka. Then even if we don't have electric lights or charcoal, we won't be inconvenienced the least bit.

Of course! If nobody else invents it, I'll invent it! That'll make Mother happy; she's always short of money to pay for electricity and charcoal. Not only Mother. Everybody in the whole world will probably be very glad, too.

That settles it! I'm going to study hard and invent an artificial sun.

Oh, by the way, I had another dream. This one was a scary one.

It was evening, and I found myself in a classroom at school. The teacher wasn't there, but Tanaka was, and Itō, and Kawakami . . . it seemed all the boys were. They were all jabbering away and the classroom was noisy. Then there was this pounding of feet outside. The pounding was not in any regular pattern. I raced to the windows and looked out. All the other kids ran

ドーッとかけよった。

　外は、たいへんなありさまだった。だって、校庭を何百匹という大犬がかけているのだ。口をあけて、するどい歯を出して、長い舌をたらしてフッフッと言ってかけている犬がいた。長い尻尾を後ろにひきずって、ピンと耳を立てて、目をいからせてかけてる犬がいた。どれも、足が長くて、せいが高くて、毛があらくて、色はちゃかっ色だった。それが、洪水のように、西の方からきて、東の方へかけて行く、後からも後からもドンドンつづいてくる。だれ一人声を出す者がなかった。みんな窓にしがみつくようにしていた。そのうち、田中くんが、

「すごいなぁ。」

と言った。すると、

「こりゃ、ヤマイヌだ。」

　川上が言った。

「どうしてオオカミなんだ。」

　伊藤がききかえした。

「みんな口が耳までさけているだろう。あれは人をくうオオカミの口だ。」

「ふーん。」

　みんなは、うなるような声を出した。ぼくはおそろし

to the windows, too. All together, like a stampede.

What we saw was really something. Hundreds of big dogs were running through the schoolyard. The dogs were running with mouths open, their sharp teeth showing and long tongues hanging down, and they were panting hard. Their long tails were dragging on the ground, their ears were standing straight up, and their eyes were blazing angrily. They were long-legged and tall-backed, and their fur was rough and greenish-brown. They came like a flood from the west and ran towards the east. One after another, one after another they came in a steady stream. Not one of us said a word. We were all pressed up against the windows.

After a while Tanaka said, "Wow!! Isn't that something!!"

Then Kawakami said, "Those are wolves!!"

"What makes you think they're wolves?" asked Itō.

"See how their mouths go all the way to their ears? Those are the mouths of man-eating wolves."

"Ooooh." Everyone let out a groan. I was scared;

くて、寒くなり、体がふるえだした。歯をじっとかみしめようと思うのに、上と下とが、がちがちかみあった。

ぼくは思った。

「オオカミは、日本では動物園にしかいなかったと教わったのになぁ。」

しかしその時、だれかが大声で言うのが聞こえた。

「戸をしめろっ。中へ入って来るぞ。」

ぼくたちは、窓のガラス戸を、がたがたたおした。四、五人は両方の入り口のひき戸の所にかけより、それをしめて、力いっぱいおさえた。

それから、何十分たったか知らない。大分時間がたった。

やはり、そとのオオカミの大群はつづいていた。すると、どこかでサイレンが鳴りだした。はんしょうもうたれだした。ぼくは、いよいよ心細くなった。

その時、入り口の戸を、外からわれるようにたたく音がした。みんな顔を見合わせた。

「先生だ。先生だ。」

と言う者があった。

「ううん、オオカミかも知れないじゃないか。」

と言う者もあった。

a chill went up my spine and I started shaking. I tried to clamp my teeth shut, but they kept chattering.

I thought to myself, "But they taught us in school that in Japan wolves are found only in zoos!"

Just then I heard someone shout, "Shut the doors! They're coming inside!"

We banged the windows shut. A handful of boys ran to the two sliding doors and shut them, pushing against them so they couldn't be opened. How many minutes passed after this, I don't know, but it was quite some time. The horde of wolves outside continued to come. Then a siren started to sound somewhere. The fire-alarm bell started ringing, too. I got more scared than ever.

Then there was someone pounding on the door from the other side, pounding so hard we thought the door would break. We all looked at one another.

"The teacher, it's the teacher," someone said.

"No, it might be wolves!" said another.

「だれですか。」

　ふるえ声で、田中くんが言った。

「けいかんだ。町のけいかんだ。」

　その声が言った。

「おい、おまわりさんだ。あけてやれよう。」

　だれかが言った。それで、戸があいて、一人の大人が入って来た。その人はカーキ色の服を着ていた。しかし、どうもへんな服だった。そして、はなの下に長いひげをはやしていた。頭のかみもボウボウのばしていた。とにかく、きみのわるい、へんちくりんなおまわりさんだった。それに、げたなんかもはいていた。

　その人は教壇に上がると、

「ただ今、けいほうが発せられました。」

　そう言うのだ。

「オオカミの一群は日本中部アルプスのけいこくから発して、マツモト、スワ、コウフの諸都市をおそい、只今トウキョウに向かうとちゅうにあります。その数何十万あるか分かりません。今では大体、三群に分かれて移動しておりますが、北アルプス、南アルプス地方の山谷にも、百、二百とほえたけって、集合しつつあるようすが見うけられますので、それらがいくつかの大群となっ

"Who is it?" asked Tanaka in a shaky voice.

"A police officer. A police officer from town," the voice said.

"Hey, it's a policeman! Open up!" said someone. Then the door opened and a man came in. He was wearing a khaki-coloured uniform. But it was a strange-looking uniform. And he had a long moustache under his nose. His hair, too, was long and wild. Anyway, he was a creepy-sort-of, strange-sort-of-looking policeman. And another thing, he had on wooden clogs, would you believe it!

He stepped up onto the teacher's platform, and said:

A warning has just been issued. A pack of wolves setting off from gorges in the Central Japanese Alps have attacked the cities of Matsumoto, Suwa, and Kōfu, and they are now headed for Tokyo. It is not known how many hundreds of thousands they number. At present they have split up and are moving in roughly three packs, but because sightings have been made of groups of a hundred to two hundred of them gathering in howling masses in the mountains as well as valleys of the Northern Alps and Southern Alps regions, it is anticipated that these groupings will form into a number of large hordes and take part in

て、どこかの村や町、あるいは市をしゅうげきに出かけ
ることは、予想されているところで、ナガノ市、ナゴヤ
市、いずれもげんじゅうなけいかいをいたしておりま
す。」

　そう言った時、だれかが手をあげてきいた。
「先生、オオカミは人を取って食うんですか。」

　すると、そのけいかんは、
「いや、そんな報告はまだ来ておりません。」

　そう言う。
「では、なぜ、町に出て来るんですか。」
「うん、それは人間があまり山の木を切りすぎたでなぁ、
オオカミも住む所がなくなったんだ。ええ、くそっとい
うわけで、やけになって出て来たとみえる。」

「それで、オオカミはどうしようというんですか。」
「うん、それじゃって、それが分からないんだ。それで
困っとるんじゃ。」

「それでは、木のある所へ移動してるんですか。」
「そうかも知れない。とにかく、薪がない。すみがない。
家をたてる。で、山をぼうずにしてしまったからな。そ
うさえしなければ、よかったんだ。困った事だ。」

　その人はすっかりしょげて、教壇の机の上にひじをつ

86

assaults on some villages and towns, or even cities, somewhere. For this reason, both Nagano City and Nagoya City are taking strict precautions.

When he finished, someone raised a hand and asked, "Sir, do the wolves catch and eat people?"

To this the policeman replied, "No, no such reports have come in yet."

"Then why do they come into the towns?"

"Because people have cut down too many of the trees in the forests, and places where the wolves can live have disappeared. It seems they could not stand this any longer and in desperation have come down out of the forests."

"Well, if that's so, what are the wolves planning to do?"

"Er, that's what we don't know. That's why we don't know what to do."

"Well, are they moving to places where there are trees?"

"Could be. Anyway, this all happened because people don't have firewood, people don't have charcoal, people want to build houses. And so they cut the trees down from the mountains and strip the mountains bare. If only they hadn't done this everything would've been all right. Now look at the mess we're in!"

With a look of complete dejection, the man put his elbows on the teacher's desk and cradled

いて、手をひたいに当ててしまった。

　その次、しかしぼくは飛び上がるほど、びっくりした。だって、教室には、いつのまにか一人もいなくなってしまっていた。そして教壇の先生の机の上には、一匹のオオカミがよこになって寝ていた。

「わーっ。」

　と言って、ぼくは大声をあげた。それで目がさめた。おそろしいゆめだった。でも、ゆめでよかった。ほんとうだったら、それこそぼくは、オオカミに食われてしまっていたかも知れない。

　朝になって、おかあさんにその話をして、ほんとうにそんな事があるか聞いてみた。おかあさんは笑っておられた。それで、ぼくはやっぱり、そんな事はないのだと思った。

his head in his hands.

The next thing, I was so startled I jumped. Y'see, all of a sudden there was nobody else in the classroom with me. And there on top of the teacher's desk at the front of the room was a wolf, lying on its side, asleep.

"Heeelp!" I screamed.

Then I woke up. It had been a terrifying dream. But good thing it was a dream. If it had been real, then for sure I might've been eaten up by that wolf.

That morning, I told Mother about my dreams, and I asked her if something like that could really happen. Mother was smiling. So I figured it was just as I'd thought, nothing like that could ever happen.